THE PEPPER PARTY

Picks the Perfect Pet

THE PEPPER PARTY IS JUST GETTING STARTED!

THE PEPPER PARTY

Picks the Perfect Pet

BY

JAY COOPER

Scholastic Inc.

For Laura, the brains and the heart
of the whole operation . . .

All rights reserved. Published by Scholastic Inc., *Publishers since 1920*. SCHOLASTIC and associated logos are trademarks and/or registered trademarks of Scholastic Inc.

ISBN 978-1-338-29702-7

10 9 8 7 6 5 4 3 2 1   19 20 21 22 23
Printed in the U.S.A.   40
First printing 2019
Book design by Nina Goffi and Christopher Stengel

CHAPTER 1

Saturdays at the Pepper house were *crazypants*.

It was the only day of the week when every member of the large Pepper family was home at the same time. They were always up to something, but on Saturdays, the Peppers of San Pimento were up to a *whole lot* of somethings all at the same time.

This Saturday
was no different:

1. Ricky Pepper (age 12) Jamming on his electric oboe
2. Beta Max Pepper (age 9) Holding auditions
3. Maria Pepper (age 9 plus 2 minutes) Prepping for the debate team
4. Meemaw Pepper (ancient) Pretending she can hear Maria
5. Tee Pepper (Mom) Getting Scoochy ready for a playdate
6. Scoochy (age 2) Not cooperating (as usual)
7. Megs Pepper (age 10) Hosting a soccer tournament for her besties
8. Sal Pepper (Dad) Perfecting his chili recipe
9. Annie Pepper (age 8) Being quiet . . . too quiet

In the upstairs hall, Megs and her pals kicked and headbutted their soccer ball down the long hallway. Just before the ball went crashing through an upstairs window, it pinged around the hallway like a pinball, then knocked the senses out of one of the kids lined up outside of her brother Beta's room.

"YOWCH!" the unfortunate boy yelled.

"Sorry, my bad!" Megs called back.

The boy grumbled and turned back to read the loose-leaf paper taped to Beta's door:

AUDITIONS TODAY!!!!!!
for
BETA MAX PEPPER'S
NEWEST, BLOOD CURDLING,
UNBELIEVABLY GROSS
HORROR FILM!

Beta, the budding director, was having actors read a scene from his (currently untitled) horror movie. The actors were supposed to act like a giant monster was eating them, which involved lots of screaming and flailing and yelling things like "Noooo! That was my favorite arm!" and "Aw man, I just bought that shirt yesterday!" But he had to keep asking them to "SPEAK UP!" because of the loud music that was leaking through the ceiling.

Upstairs, the eldest Pepper kid, Ricky, was thrashing away on his electric oboe. That's right. Electric oboe. (He'd been playing sad songs for over a week now, ever since his girlfriend dumped him on the last day of camp.) Ricky's songs had titles like "How Can I Canoe without You?" and "You've Stomped Out the Campfire in My Heart." Somehow the electric oboe made a normally sad song a whole lot sadder.

Meanwhile, their sister Maria Pepper practiced a speech for the debate team on her ancient grandmother Meemaw in the den. Yes, it was the middle of summer, and *yes*, her debate subject, "Pencils vs. Pens (Who's Really Number Two?)," was still months away, but Maria liked to be extra prepared. The only problem was that Meemaw was nearly deaf and kept shouting "WHAT? WHAT?" every time Maria made a point.

In the kitchen, the kids' dad, Sal, added spice to a simmering pot of chili. He tasted it. *Needs some paprika . . . or is it peppermint?* he wondered. He was always adding things to his chili. Their father didn't consider himself so much a chili expert as a chili *inventor*. Sal just knew that this was the year he would finally win the annual San Pimento Chili Cook-Off.

The smell of chili made Tee Pepper's stomach grumble as she tried to ready the littlest Pepper for a playdate. But toddlers like Scoochy prefer using their pants as a pirate flag to actually wearing them.

There was always a lot going on in the Pepper house.

But this Saturday, there was one exception.

CHAPTER 2

Annie Pepper's room was silent.

Annie was the second youngest of the six Pepper kids, and she hadn't made so much as a peep the entire day. A Pepper without a peep is rather a rarity, but with this Pepper it was practically unheard of. Annie was the kind of kid who was always hard at work on some sort of crazy plan. On a day like today, you might find her peddling do-it-yourself lemonade to people on the street (which was really just selling lemons from the grocery store for twice the price), or opening an amateur detective agency with her friends, or searching for gold with the help of an old treasure map, something like that . . . Instead she sat on her bed, quiet as a mouse, reading and rereading a flyer her friend Marco had given her.

This was because Annie had realized something the day before—something really huge.

She had been zipping down the sidewalk on her bicycle, enjoying the sunny summer day. Having already circled the block a few times, she was relishing some wind-blowing-through-her-ponytail action when she spotted what looked like a moving carpet coming her way.

And it was moving quickly.

Annie hit the brakes with a squeal. As the strange carpet got closer, she realized it wasn't a carpet at all . . . it was squirrels. Dozens and dozens of squirrels. A furry sea of them flowed over the grass. They were chasing something small and tan.

Whatever it was, the squirrels were gaining on it, and they seemed to have vengeance in their eyes.

Annie wasn't sure what to do. Should she flee? Should she fight? Before she could decide, the tiny thing the squirrels were chasing made a beeline right for her and leapt, first onto the wheel of her bike, and then straight into her basket.

It was, unbelievably, a Chihuahua. A small, short-haired dog, with big, beady, and frankly frightened-out-of-its-mind eyes.

The squirrels were almost on them now. Before she could think, Annie turned the bike around and peeled out of there quick.

Three of the squirrels managed to leap onto her back wheel guard, but Annie nudged them off with her sneaker. "No hitchhikers!" she yelled.

When the rodents finally disappeared on the horizon, Annie came to a stop and looked at the pooch. The poor little thing was shaking like crazy. She hugged him tight.

Then she heard a shout from behind her. "Oh, (huff) dude! Is (huff) Azzie okay???"

It was her friend Marco running down the block. He stopped in front of her and then put his hands on his knees and wheezed.

She nodded toward the short-haired ball of shaking nerves in her arms. "Marco, is this little cutie *yours*?"

Marco held up a finger, the universal symbol for "give-me-a-minute-to-catch-my-breath-or-I-might-die-right-here-on-this-sidewalk-okay?"

When he could finally continue, he said, "Mine? Nah, this is Azzie. He's from my aunt's animal shelter. I got a summer job there. She pays me a dollar to walk them, and a dollar to bring 'em back. You saved me a dollar there. Thanks!"

"What happened?" Annie asked.

"Well, we were walking, and Azzie started barking and lunging at these two dumb squirrels. Chihuahuas and squirrels are natural enemies, you know. They got their squirrel buddies and cornered us on Seeley Street. Azzie got loose and bolted. Man, you wouldn't think a dog so small could run so fast!"

Annie looked down in wonder at the tiny, shivering Chihuahua. She thought he might be just about the most pathetic creature in the whole world. She looked into those big, brown, fidgety eyes, and just like that, fell madly in love.

Annie walked with Marco and Azzie back to the shelter. It was in an outdoor mall and had a bright pink sign that read:

When Marco opened the door, Annie could hear squawks, barks, and meows coming from inside. He came back and handed Annie a Frida Flamingo's Fun Facts flyer. It was full of information about the shelter and pictures of animals available for adoption . . . including Azzie.

"I also get a nickel for every flyer I hand out," Marco said. "Who knows, maybe your mom or dad will let you adopt him?"

Annie looked at the pamphlet dreamily. *Adopt Azzie? Yeah, sure*, she thought. *And maybe monkeys will dance in their underpants.*

But as Annie biked home, she couldn't get the image of the pup out of her head. She imagined taking him to the park (even if those squirrels came back) or to the beach (though it's possible he'd be frightened of crabs, too) or even just lounging at home (of course, her father might mistake him for a chili ingredient). They would go somewhere together, she was sure, and it would be the most amazing thing ever.

Now it was Saturday, and dinner was fast approaching. Annie had spent the day sitting on her bed, reading Frida Flamingo's Fun Facts and staring hopelessly at the photo of Azzie. The poor little guy didn't have a home, and Annie was more than willing to give him the best one ever. No pet owner in the history of pet owners would be as devoted as she would be. There was just one problem—one gigantic, enormous, Godzilla-sized problem. Many a Pepper kid had tried to bring an animal home, and every Pepper had failed.

They had begged, cajoled, and cried, but their dad would always cross his arms, shake his head, and say, "Peppers don't do pets."

But not this time.

Annie had decided that she would do just about anything to adopt Azzie. No Pepper rule was going to stand between her and her love.

This Pepper wasn't taking no for an answer.

CHAPTER 3

Dinner in the Pepper household was an every-Pepper-for-him-or-herself kind of affair. The table was crowded with bowls of mashed potatoes (the kids fought over the first scoop), crispy pan-fried pork chops (they fought over the biggest chop), and of course a number of healthy vegetables (no one fought over these).

But that night Annie took a large helping of green beans and an even larger one of Brussels sprouts with a smile.

Her mother was immediately suspicious. Her brothers and sisters were, too.

"What's with all the veggies?" Maria asked as she delicately cut into her pork chop. "Are you becoming a vegetarian?" Maria didn't like that idea. Being socially and environmentally conscious was *her* thing.

Beta looked up from the potato volcano with butter lava he was sculpting. "Were you bitten by a radioactive rabbit? Are you mutating into a human-bunny hybrid?" His eyes widened. He'd have to remember that for his movie.

"Mmwff wmmmf?" Scoochy spat mashed potato bits everywhere.

Annie wiped a glob of potato from her cheek and tried to sound grown-up. "I just think that trying to eat healthier is the *responsible* thing to do. I'm a very *responsible* person, you know."

Their mother smiled. "Oh, are you?"

"Yeah, Annie's responsible for half the messes in this house!" Megs laughed.

Annie did her best to remain calm and not fling potatoes into her sister's hair. "You know who's not responsible?"

"Who, kiddo?" asked Sal.

"People who abandon pets. Nearly seven million pets are abandoned every year in the United States!"

"That's terrible," said her mother as she cut some pork for Scoochy.

"You know who *else* isn't responsible?" Annie continued.

"Hmmm?" asked their father, who was now peppering his pork chops and applesauce. (Sal Pepper was a man who added spice to everything, even his milkshakes.)

"Families that *could* adopt a pet and don't. Only three million of those seven million pets are adopted each year."

"That's awful!" This was from Megs, who was listening attentively. Suddenly Annie realized that she had everyone's attention, even Scoochy's, and the Scooch never listened to anything.

"Great googly-moogly! Where have you been learning these terrible things?" asked Sal.

"I'd sure like to know," said Tee. Like all mothers, Tee could predict trouble—and her senses were tingling.

Annie pulled out the flyer and placed it on the table.

"My friend Marco is spending the summer working at a shelter. It's full of animals that need good homes."

Her siblings stared at the flyer in wonder. This was something they hadn't tried when they'd asked if they could have a pet. They had cried. Bribed. Maria had even blackmailed their dad

once. But none of them had tried actual *cold, hard facts*!

Sal picked up the flyer. "Frida Flamingo's Animal Adoption Agency?" He smiled and put it back down. "You know the rule, Annie. *Peppers don't do pets!*"

But Annie wasn't about to give up after

just one try. She grabbed the flyer from her dad and began to read aloud. "'Every year three million cats and four million dogs end up homeless. And it's not just dogs and cats. Rabbits, hamsters, mice, and tortoises . . . the list goes on and on. At Frida Flamingo's Animal Adoption Agency, we care for as many as we can. *But we can't do it by ourselves.* Won't you lend a paw?'"

Then Annie pointed at the photo of Azzie. "Isn't our family motto 'Peppers always protect'?"

Tee sighed. "The Peppers have *a lot* of mottoes. Your father comes up with three or four a day." This was true. Sal Pepper's favorite motto was: "With a good motto, you can do anything!"

The family passed around the flyer, and it finally made its way to their mother. She looked at the dozens of sad animal faces, and her heart crumbled. Sal had seen them, too. There were tears in his big brown eyes, and his mustache was quivering.

Sal and Tee hadn't realized it yet, but Annie had already won.

CHAPTER 4

"And who exactly is going to walk this pet?" their mother asked.

"We'll all take turns! Right, guys?" Annie pleaded. Her brothers and sisters nodded enthusiastically.

"And the poop? Animals do poop, you know. A lot!"

"We'll pick up the poop!" Beta cried cheerfully. "It will be our number-one priority!"

"And our *number-two* priority." Megs winked.

"So you say." Tee crossed her arms and scowled.

Then Ricky spoke, his voice dark and heartbroken. "What if we make a solemn vow? One you can't break. Like when you promise to write someone after camp ends, *and you make a solemn vow*, then you are absolutely bound to keep your promise."

"You'll *all* take this vow?" Tee asked.

The kids nodded vigorously.

"Fine. Everyone raise your right hand and repeat after me."

They all raised a hand.

"I didn't mean you, Sal!"

Sal quickly put his hand behind his back. He grinned sheepishly.

"The Pepper kids promise to take good care of whatever pet we adopt. To *wash* him. To *walk* him. *To pick up his poop.* We so solemnly swear."

All the kids said, "WE SO SOLEMNLY SWEAR!"

Then they all cheered and high-fived. Annie could imagine bringing Azzie home. They would coo over his big Chihuahua eyes, and his adorable shivers, and his . . .

"Oooh! Can we get a cat?" Maria asked suddenly.

Beta gave her a shove. "Are you kidding me? Mom finally lets us get a pet, and you want to waste it on a boring old *cat*? No way! It should be something interesting! Something . . . filmable!"

"We should get a dog!"

"We should get a cat!"

"We should get . . . the hat," Sal said excitedly.

NO! thought Annie angrily. *It was my idea! I should get to pick!*

Tee cried, "Not that hat!"

Sal jumped up from the table. "Yes! The hat!" He ran out of the room. A few minutes later Sal returned with an old, worn top hat. He

blew a cloud of dust off it. "I present the hat of your great-grandfather, Presto Pepper!"

Tee groaned. The hat was never a good idea.

Presto Pepper loomed large in Pepper family history. He was famous for being the worst magician of the twentieth century. He was so bad that people actually came to his shows to see him screw up. (He could only ever make things partly disappear. Once he'd sawed his assistant in half, and it took a week to clean up the mess.)

But as bad a magician as Presto was, he was an even worse decision maker! He had twelve children, and they always wanted their own way. So whenever the family made a big decision, they drew names from his hat. This meant that occasionally a two-year-old decided where the family would go on vacation or what kind of car they should buy (for years they drove a fire truck), but dear old Presto always stood by the decision. Fair was fair, and the tradition lived on.

Sal placed the hat on the table with a flourish.

Tee reluctantly got some scraps of paper and wrote one of the kids' names on each of them, all the while muttering things like "ridiculous tradition" and "can't believe we're doing this silly hat thing again!" All except Scoochy, who couldn't be trusted. Two-year-olds are people, but even family rules had limits.

Sal pretended not to hear her. He took the slips of paper from her with a smile, threw them into the hat, and shook it. "The Presto Pepper rule says the eldest Pepper gets to pick. Meemaw, that's you."

"WHAT? WHAT?" croaked their grand-mother. "I can't hear a word you're saying!"

Sal yelled in her ear, "I SAID PICK A NAME FROM THE HAT, MEEMAW!"

"All right! You don't have to shout! I got EARS, y'know!" their grandmother grumbled as she reached into the hat and pulled out a slip. She handed it to Sal.

"It looks like the Pepper who will pick the family pet is . . ."

"Let it be me. Please, please let it be me!" Annie whispered to herself.

She closed her eyes.

She bit her lip.

She crossed her fingers.

". . . Beta Max Pepper!"

Rats! Annie thought to herself.

CHAPTER 5

Long before Frida Flamingo opened her animal adoption agency, she was a movie star. She still dressed as though she were going in front of the camera. And today she had quite an audience. There were Peppers everywhere: They peeked into birdcages, watched hamsters run the wheel, and recoiled from coiled snakes. They petted

the dogs and stroked the cats. Scoochy even tried to eat a fish.

Annie ran straight to Azzie's cage. He scampered across his pen to her and shivered hello. She called excitedly to her brother, "Don't you just love him, Beta? Isn't he the *cutest*? His name is Azzie."

Beta raised a critical eyebrow. "Hmm. He doesn't seem very . . . camera ready. I'm gonna take a look around."

Annie groaned.

After looking at all the animals, Beta walked up to Frida. "Excuse me, miss. Do you have anything less . . . *regular*?"

Frida raised an eyebrow. "Child," she began, "all my animals have *flair*. All my animals have *panache*!" She slung her feather boa over her shoulder and smiled. "But perhaps you are looking for something a bit more . . . exotic. Hmmm?"

Beta smiled, "YEAH! Like maybe something caught in the depths of the Amazon jungle or in the Himalayan mountains!"

"I see. YES. I know just the thing! I'll be right back!"

Before leaving the room, she turned to Beta. "Young man, you remind me of the famous movie director Stevie Shpealburger. I got him his first job, you know, as an errand boy back at Looniversal Pictures. Ah, those were the days!" She swept through a beaded curtain and returned with a plastic cage.

Frida placed it on the counter and opened the top.

The Peppers crowded around.

A single hairy leg slowly extended from the shadows. That leg was followed by another and another and another and still more!

There were eight hairy legs in total, surrounding a furry body, large scary jaws, and a whole bunch of eyeballs!

Frida Flamingo had a tarantula.

"SPIDEY!" cheered Scoochy.

KLIK!

Beta's eyes grew big. The tarantula was horrible. It was gross. It was . . . *perfect*!

"This is Harry. He's quite the sweetie pie, don't you think?"

"He's gonna be a star!" Beta yelled.

Annie's jaw dropped. She got her parents to agree to adopt a pet, and they ended up with a tarantula? Ugh. Strike that: *Double* ugh!

Still, Annie hadn't given up quite yet. She quickly grabbed Azzie from his cage and held him up beside Harry the tarantula. "Think about

 it, Beta. This one is cute, and cuddly, and adorable, and this one is a gigantic spider that could gnaw your face off in your sleep!"

Beta grinned happily. "EXACTLY!" He hugged the tarantula's terrarium.

Annie slumped.

At first Tee put her foot down: This monster was most certainly not coming home with them. But Sal reminded her that, while he agreed with her that a tarantula was a terrifically terrible idea for a family pet, according to the Pepper family rules, Beta got to choose. And Beta had chosen Harry.

The other kids looked depressed as their parents signed all the forms and paid the adoption fee. Frida handed Beta a bag of live crickets (apparently tarantulas ate *live* food—when Maria heard this, she turned a sickly shade of green and had to go outside for some fresh air). Sal purchased a plastic terrarium to house Harry.

Beta was over the moon. He had finally

found a monster for his movie. Looking at Harry, the perfect title popped into his head: *Terrorus, Tarantula from beyond the Stars!* As soon as he and Harry got home, Beta would begin writing his masterpiece.

Annie was in tears as she gently returned Azzie to his cage. "Don't worry. I'll find a way to adopt you," she whispered to him. "I promise." Azzie licked up a teardrop that clung to the end of Annie's nose.

CHAPTER 6

No one minded Harry staying in Beta's room. Even so, Beta took him on trips to the mall, on playdates, even to church.

But mostly he took Harry to the backyard to film his monster movie. He built a town using Ricky's old model railroad set, complete with stores, trees, and even tiny plastic

townspeople. When Beta filmed Harry crawling over the model town and then edited in real
actors on his computer, it looked as though a
giant alien spider was really invading the earth!

One of Beta's favorite scenes was in a night-
club. He dressed his friends up as a bunch of
dancers with seventies hair and gold chains.
As Terrorus slowly tore the roof off the club,
only one dancer realized their danger and
pointed up in silent shock at the monster over
and over. But all the other dancers thought it
was just a cool new dance move and copied
him . . . that is, until Terrorus ate them all up
with disco music playing in the background. It
was great!

But it was only great for Beta. Every time Annie watched her brother happily film the so-called family pet, she got a little bit angrier. *What a joke*, she thought. Beta hadn't even thought for a moment that the rest of them weren't nearly as keen on the idea of a pet tarantula as he was. *Selfish, that's what it is*, she thought.

One night, after a long day of filming, Beta tried to bring Harry to the dinner table.

He bobbed his curly head excitedly as he placed the terrarium beside his plate. Maria and Annie, already at the table, screamed in horror.

"Oh, grow up," Beta complained. "He's just a harmless old spider."

"Nothing about that tarantula seems harmless to me," said Maria.

Annie agreed with her sister. "I can't believe you got us an animal that we can't even touch! That's why they're called pets. You're supposed to *pet* them."

Megs leaned in and laughed and lightly poked the cage. "Awww, I think that he's kind of cute, in a gross, spidery sorta way!"

"Uh-uh. No way," said Tee, entering the room and wagging her finger. "No spiders at the table. Shoo!"

"Aw, nuts. C'mon, Harry. Let's go get you some nice, tasty crickets for dinner!" Beta trudged out of the dining room with his movie star. Annie watched him go, burning with anger that her brother had picked a pet for himself, and not for the family.

Later that night, after everyone had gone to bed, Annie crept quietly out of the room she shared with Maria. She tiptoed down the hall and peeked into Beta's room. He'd fallen asleep at his computer and was snoring lightly.

Harry the tarantula skittered around his terrarium. Annie walked over and made a face at the spider. It was only a matter of time before her parents realized that adopting Harry was a terrible mistake. He belonged with a nice Goth family or a motorcycle gang. He was definitely *not* the right pet for the Peppers. She just needed her parents to understand that sooner rather than later.

An idea came to her.

Maybe she could speed the process along.

All it took was opening the terrarium door.

CHAPTER 7

Annie lay in bed all night regretting what she'd done. Her stomach felt queasy and her heart would not stop racing. But it wasn't just that. Every time she started to drift off to sleep, she felt fuzzy legs climbing all over her. By morning, Annie hadn't slept a wink.

She yawned, dressed, and headed for the den.

For the rest of the family, it was a typical morning. Sal had already dropped off Megs at lacrosse practice and was driving his food truck, the  Chili Chikka-Wow-Wow, over to the board-walk, where he would spend the day selling his delicious chili and, of course, perfecting his recipe for the annual San Pimento Chili Cook-Off. (*Maybe it needs more mayonnaise, or possibly popcorn*, he wondered.) Tee had just finished her morning run and was enjoying a long, hot bath. Ricky wrote a sad love song on the couch, which he titled "I Need S'more of Your Love." Maria sat next to him and read a book titled: *How to Make Friends, Influence People, and Crush Your Enemies into Dust*. Scoochy hooted happily at the latest episode of *Sesame Street*, but Meemaw only grumbled about those puppets needing to speak up.

Suddenly, Beta ran into the room, looking sweaty and scared.

"Has anyone seen Harry???"

Maria put her book down slowly. "And *why* would we have seen your spider, goofball?"

Beta's eyes were wide with fear. "Because." He swallowed hard. "Harry is missing!"

～～～～～～～

Harry the tarantula had been enjoying a pleasant stroll around the house. He was super excited about his new family, especially that redheaded kid who kept calling him "a star." But the kid needed to calm down. Even stars needed a break now and then.

HARRY'S EVENING EXPLORATIONS

TOP FLOOR

ATTIC

BOTTOM FLOOR

So Harry had visited every room in the whole house, and boy, had he worked up a thirst!

Crawling down the hallway, he heard a tap running. *Aha*, Harry thought, *water*.

He pushed open the bathroom door with one gigantic hairy leg and crept into the room. He was happily surprised to find the kid's mother relaxing in the bathtub. *Perfect!* He could have a drink *and* introduce himself at the same time! Harry's own mother had always said that Harry was the most polite tarantula she had raised. He wanted to make a good impression.

The tarantula began to slowly climb up the bathtub. He made his way around the tub's edge. Eventually he got close enough to reach out a leg and lightly nudge the mother's cheek.

He clicked a happy "Hello!" and smiled at her with his giant tarantula jaws.

"YAAAAAAAAHHHHHHHHH!!!!!!!!!"

Tee Pepper screamed so loud, every kid in the house heard her.

She screamed so loud, everyone on the block heard her. Miles away, Sal Pepper heard her scream as he was setting up his food truck. In fact, Tee Pepper screamed *so* loud that a scientist with a gigantic satellite dish in Brazil who was searching the sky for proof of alien life recorded her scream and checked off a box that read: *maybe*.

Later that day, a teary Beta handed the plastic terrarium with Harry inside it back to Frida Flamingo.

"Well," she sighed. "It's unfortunate, but I *do* understand. A tarantula isn't for everyone. In fact, they're for nearly no one. They are what we call in show biz an *acquired* taste."

"Just like those crickets. Blech!" agreed Maria.

Frida Flamingo stared down her glasses at Sal and Tee Pepper. "However, we don't have a money back policy. Exchange only."

Sal smiled. "That's okay!" He pulled out the battered old top hat. Tee put her head in her hands.

"Now, according to Presto Pepper's rules, in the rare event of a second pull, the next oldest Pepper picks! That would be me!" Sal dipped his hand into the hat and rustled the papers around.

Annie scrunched her eyes closed and wished with all her might that she would get to pick the next pet. She was sure that once Beta got to know Azzie, he'd never miss that creepy spider anyway. Still, she felt pretty awful about what she had done. She had avoided her brother's eyes all day.

"Here we go," said Sal as he dug around in the hat. He pulled out a slip of paper and examined it. Unfortunately it was actually *two* slips. One had wrapped itself around the other.

"Fiddle-faddle!" Tee said. "You'll have to do it again."

Sal shook his head. "Not according to the

bylaws. Both slips are valid. Peppers don't do do-overs."

Megs laughed and whispered to Maria, "Dad just said *doo doo!*"

Maria nudged her hard in the ribs. "Such a child," she grumbled.

"I don't believe it." Tee shook her head.

Sal reached into the hat and pulled out a long, yellowing scroll. "Here it is. Rule eighteen, subsection C: Peppers don't do do-overs. Even if multiple slips of paper are accidentally pulled from the hat." He stuck out his tongue, rolled up the paper, and put it back inside the hat.

"Dad said *doo doo* again!"

Tee threw her hands up in the air. "Okay. Fine. Whatever!" She read the slips of paper. "Ricky and Maria. Pick a pet."

Annie couldn't believe her ears. *TWO* names from the hat, and she still wasn't one of them??? *It's just not fair*, she thought, trying to hide the tears welling up in her eyes.

But Ricky and Maria couldn't decide on the same pet. So the family ended up with two new members of the Pepper family.

Maria picked a dignified white cat, complete with a bell tied with pink ribbon around her neck. Lacey had the grace of a French countess.

Ricky's heart melted when he discovered a sad lovebird named Elvis. The bird had been in a funk since losing his partner earlier that year. Frida

said that Elvis had once
burned with love, but
now he barely pecked
at his food, and he
would not sing or
swing his hips at all
anymore.

The only thing that
seemed to interest him was a tiny blue suede
pillow that smelled of his lost love. Frida
explained that Elvis's mate had liked to be
spritzed with a flowery perfume called "Hunka
Hunka Burnin' Lavender."

Ricky looked deep into Elvis's sad bird eyes.
"I'm taking you home. We'll get through this
together."

Frida leaned down and whispered to Beta,
"What's his deal?"

"Summer camp heartbreak," Beta whispered back.

"Yowch! Those are the worst." Frida dabbed her eyes with the tip of her feather boa.

Beta took a long look at her. Frida Flamingo looked like someone who had lived a life. "Did you *really* discover Stevie Shpealburger?"

CHAPTER 8

As upset as Annie was over her terrible luck, at least this time the family had ended up with normal pets.

Lacey the cat was beautiful and poised. Frida said she had belonged to a famous French ballet dancer. Lacey certainly acted very French. She wouldn't so much curl up in your lap as she would pirouette into it, *oui?* And she turned up her nose at any food that wasn't Parisian, which meant Sal had to constantly churn out crepes and soufflés to keep her happy.

Elvis wasn't scary like Harry, but he was *very* depressing. The lovebird's favorite hobby was swinging limply in his cage. His second-favorite hobby was sobbing, like a hound dog crying all the time. Elvis was utterly and completely heartbroken, which was fine with Ricky, since he was utterly and completely heartbroken, too. Ricky tried playing the electric oboe for the bird, which helped a little.

Sometimes Elvis would even sway slightly to the music. But each time he remembered his lost love, Priscilla, he would slump into his birdseed, and Ricky would flop onto his bed, reminded of the girlfriend who had broken his heart. Ricky's room was a regular heartbreak hotel.

As for Beta, he hadn't given up on his movie after losing Harry. Instead, in a flash of inspiration, he filmed clips of Lacey and Elvis and edited them together with footage of Harry in order to continue the project. He'd decided that Terrorus could be a giant mutant combination of animals: part spider, part cat, and part bird! Neither Lacey nor Elvis was as brilliant on camera as Harry, however. Lacey seemed bored all the time, and Beta had to prop Elvis up with tied string in order to make him "fly." Elvis was just too down in the dumps to do it on his own.

Annie was worried that if Elvis stayed depressed, her parents might decide he was a bad influence on her brother and try to get rid of the bird. She wasn't about to let Elvis get sent back to the shelter on her watch. Not after what happened to Harry. She thought the little guy just needed some good old-fashioned cheering up. Remembering the story about his lost love, Priscilla, and her perfumed blue suede pillow, Annie snapped her fingers. *Maybe*, she thought, *if we spritz a bit of that perfume in Ricky's room, Elvis will feel all shook up again!*

As luck would have it, Sal was planning a trip to the market for some ingredients for the chili recipe he was working on for the San Pimento Chili Cook-Off. "Bananas! Bananas in chili could be . . . bananas!" He agreed to take Annie to the department store as well.

Annie returned with a small bottle of Elvis's lost love's perfume, which she placed on the dresser in her room. She planned to give it to Ricky later that evening.

At dinner that night, Sal proposed a toast. "Well, Peppers, it took us a second try, but it looks like we finally picked the perfect pet."

"Pets," Ricky corrected him sadly.

Sal chuckled and patted his son's back. Then he filled everyone's juice glasses. "Let's raise a glass to old Presto Pepper: a terrible decision maker, but a fair one!"

Everyone clinked their glasses. "To Presto!"

Meanwhile, Lacey had just been rudely woken from a teensy nap. (A cat's beauty rest was as important to her as food, water, and ignoring zee humans to let zem know how little she needed zem.) She had been lying on the hall floor like it was her own personal chaise longue. *All zee better to make zee people walk over you*, she thought.

The sound of someone giggling had Lacey's eyes shooting open just as a cloud of perfume spritzed above her! The scent of lavender in the air was so thick that she sneezed. How vile! She turned her head just in time to see a pair of tiny sneakers darting around the corner. *The problem with families*, she thought, *is too many of zee tiny people.*

Upstairs in Ricky's room, Elvis lay down on the newspaper lining his cage and promised himself he'd never sing again. *Without my baby, Priscilla, I'm just a teddy bear without any stuffin'*, he thought. *All my rhinestones are whine-stones! A-huh a-huh a-huh*, he blubbered.

But then a scent wafted by his beak. A *lav-enderish* scent.

Elvis knew that smell. *Only one lil' darlin' in the whole wide world wears that perfume*, he thought. It was Priscilla. His beaked baby doll had come back!

All at once, the bird jumped to his feet. His sagging pompadour stood at attention, and his sunglasses glistened with excitement in the attic light. His lovely lovebird had to be nearby. *I need a little less conversation, and a little more action*, he thought. He tried to squeeze through the bars of his cage, but couldn't quite fit.

Elvis wasn't about to give up. He had to make this jailhouse rock! Wrapping his wings around two of the rods, he pulled with all his birdly might. With a tiny squeal of bending metal, Elvis wrenched them apart just wide enough for him to fly through. And fly he did.

I can't help fallin' in love with you, baby! Your Elvis is on his way! he squawked happily.

Lacey was padding stealthily down the hall, hoping no one would see (or worse, smell) her, when Elvis flew around the corner. Lacey hissed, but the bird wasn't stopping.

"Mmmrrrowwwr!" she howled in fear, and ran down the stairs like a shot.

Elvis was so shook up at the return of his love that he didn't even stop to wonder why she'd lost her wings, sprouted a tail, and was five times her former size. What did it matter? His loneliness was over. He inhaled deeply—Hunka Hunka Burnin' Lavender. *Don't be cruel, darlin'*, he thought as he picked up speed.

Downstairs, Sal was on his second helping of Tee's vegetarian lasagna when he heard a low whine. His fork paused halfway to his mouth.

"What's that sound?" he asked.

Everyone shrugged.

RRRRRRRRRREEEEOOOOWWWW! SPLAT!!!!

A very white cat had landed in Sal's very red lasagna. Lacey scampered and scrabbled across the dinner table, knocking into drinks and flipping over plates.

"KITTY!" Scoochy giggled happily as Maria tried to grab the freaked-out feline. But as quickly as Lacey had landed on the table she was gone, leaving only a trail of tomato-flavored paw prints.

Elvis flew past the family like a jet. The bird had picked up enough speed that he emitted a sonic boom when he flew past, knocking over Scoochy's high chair.

WHOOOOOOOOOSH! BOOM!!!

"BIRDIE!" Scoochy clapped her hands with glee as Ricky's jaw dropped.

"Keep your claws off my cat!" Maria yelled, chasing after Elvis.

Ricky threw down his napkin and ran after her. "Don't you bully my bird!" he cried.

Sal wiped the cat hair from his forkful of lasagna and swallowed. "Wonderful dinner, hon."

Tee glared at him darkly.

Throughout the house, boy chased girl, girl chased bird, and bird chased cat. Tables were knocked over, framed pictures fell to the ground, vases shattered.

Eventually Elvis cornered Lacey by the empty fireplace in the living room. It was now or never. He flew straight at her. *Aloha, darlin'*, he thought.

Not knowing what else to do, Lacey relied on instinct . . . and opened her mouth.

When Maria and Ricky finally caught up with them, Lacey sat dazed with the bottom half of a lovebird sticking out of her mouth.

Ricky and Maria each grabbed a tiny lovebird leg and pulled before Lacey had a chance to swallow. (*Zee joke was on zem, however. Lacey would never eat anything so . . . so . . . American!*) What was left of Elvis popped out of the cat's mouth. He was now only half the bird he used to be. From the waist up, all of Elvis's feathers had come off in the cat's mouth. Lacey spat and coughed angrily.

But then Elvis caught another whiff of the perfumed cat. His eyes glazed over like a love-struck zombie, and he lunged madly at her again just as Sal and Tee entered the room.

They surveyed the knocked-over lamps, the

shattered pictures, the rain of feathers, and two of their children struggling to keep a crazy love-bird off an outraged cat. A single feather landed lightly on the tip of Sal's mustache.

This new arrangement would not do.

CHAPTER 9

"You have *got* to be kidding me." Frida stared in disbelief at the Peppers. "You say that the *bird* won't stop chasing the *cat*. Are you sure you don't have that the wrong way round?"

Sal threw his hands in the air. "He's madly in love with her. It's a mystery!" It wasn't a mystery to Annie, however. The minute she had

caught a whiff of Lacey, she had run to her room. Just as she had suspected, the bottle of perfume was missing! Someone had taken it and doused the cat! Now she felt even worse. If she hadn't bought the perfume, Elvis wouldn't be madly in love with Lacey. Now Annie was responsible for the return of THREE animals to Frida Flamingo's.

Ricky began to cry when Frida put Elvis back on the shelf with the other birds.

Frida patted Ricky on the back. "There, there. Chin up!" Then she jabbed a finger in Sal's face. "All right. I will give you. One. More. Chance. I suppose you're going to bring out that ridiculous top hat again." (Which, of course, Sal did.)

Tee was the next oldest Pepper, so she got to choose. Annie and Megs were the only two Peppers left with names in the hat, meaning Annie had an even 50 percent chance of adopting Azzie now.

Annie's mom reached in and pulled out a slip of paper. "Congratulations . . . Megs!"

Megs jumped in the air. "Woohoo!" she yelled. Then she spent the next two hours looking through Frida's shop to find her perfect match.

"Lizard? Nope. Chicken? Nope. Dodo? Interesting, but nah."

Megs walked up and down the aisle. She stopped right by Azzie the Chihuahua's cage and gasped.

"You. Are. PERFECT!!!"

For a brief second Annie thought divine intervention had steered her sporty sister toward the Chihuahua of her dreams, but then Megs opened the cage right next to Azzie's and pulled out a very cheerful-looking pig. "I dub thee . . . OINK!"

Oink, appropriately enough, oinked.

Annie wanted to cry, but Ricky was already doing that.

Oink turned out to be an adorable little pink sweetheart who loved to snuggle, especially when snacks were involved. He played fetch-the-carrot with Megs for hours, curled up on Maria's lap with a good book and an even better chocolate bar, and listened to Ricky play his oboe while nibbling an apple into the shape of a broken heart. He even let Scoochy ride around the house on his back if it meant a sugar cube afterward.

Even Annie had to admit that Oink was pretty great. She loved how he'd jump into her bed in the morning and snuffle her awake. And the cute way he'd waddle down the hall. Perhaps most of all, she loved that Beta loved Oink.

Beta had altered his movie again, making Terrorus a giant mutant *Spider-Bird-Cat-Pig from beyond the Stars!* He had put together clips of Harry, Elvis, and Lacey with new footage of Oink. To make it seamless, Beta had given Oink fake spider legs, bird wings, and a cat's tail and ears.

SPIDER LEGS

BIRD WINGS

CAT EARS

CAT TAIL (MASKING TAPE)

OINK

And Oink turned out to be a real ham. On cue, he would roar dramatically like a real movie monster. If Beta promised him a piece of cheese, he would pick up subway trains and throw them, or rampage through the tiny town Beta had built, crushing mini pedestrians under his adorable pink hooves.

While everyone played with the precious piglet, Sal continued to perfect his entry for the annual San Pimento Chili Cook-Off. He had added all sorts of crazy ingredients: oatmeal and eggplant, celery and cereal, Popsicle and paprika . . . Finally, the evening before the big day, Sal had very delicately tiptoed across the linoleum floor, and with the whole family watching from the doorway, he sprinkled one final pinch of chili powder into the giant pot of chili that he had spent the week perfecting.

He dipped a spoon into the bubbling pot and sipped, swishing the chili around like mouthwash. Then he swallowed and smacked his lips once or twice. Everyone held their breath, waiting for the results. A single tear had rolled down his cheek and onto his mustache.

"It's perfect!"

Oink watched all of this with a great deal of interest. He licked his snout.

Sal Pepper's soon-to-be-award-winning chili

just had to simmer overnight. Then it would be ready to enter into the contest. That night Sal dreamt of gold medals and chili peppers.

The next morning, their father got out of bed, put on his bathrobe and bunny slippers, and padded into the kitchen to brew some coffee. He yawned loudly as he pushed open the kitchen's swinging door.

Then he froze.

The kitchen was a disaster. Shredded cereal boxes and ripped potato chip bags littered the counter. The refrigerator door was open, its light casting an eerie glow over puddles of orange juice and milk spilled on the linoleum floor. Vegetable lo mein and half-eaten slices of pizza stuck to the walls. There was even the skeleton of an entire roasted chicken.

But that wasn't the *worst* of it.

An empty pot lay dead center on the kitchen floor, licked clean.

The most perfect chili that Sal Pepper had ever made was gone.

Sal dropped to his knees and cradled the pot in his hands. "NOOOOO!!!!!" he yelled.

This brought the whole family running into the kitchen in their pajamas.

"UH-OH," said Scoochy.

Megs bit her lip.

Annie said, "Oh brother."

Beta responded, "Why does everyone always blame me???"

Tee gasped, "Who could have done this?"

Crunch! Someone—or something—was in the pantry.

Sal grabbed a spatula and approached slowly. He crept to the darkened doorway and flipped on the light.

Sitting in the middle of the pantry floor was Oink, happily chewing a candy bar. He looked up at Sal and burped loudly. The almost-but-not-quite-award-winning chili had stained his snout.

Sal's face, normally a rosy hue, turned bright red. Soon it was purple. Then plaid. Steam poured from his ears.

"You . . . you . . . *PIG*!!!!" Sal yelled.

Oink may have been young, but he

was no dummy. With a panicked "Oink!" he hauled his curly tail out of there.

Sal lunged, but Oink darted between his legs.

What followed was the messiest chase the Pepper home had ever seen.

But as Sal scurried after Oink, his progress was slowed as Pepper kid after Pepper kid leapt onto his back, weighing him down and pleading with him to stop.

Annie, who clung to one of his shoulders, tried to talk some sense into him. "Dad! He's just a baby pig! Please don't kill Oink, Dad! PLEASE!!!"

Sal yelled, "I'm not gonna kill him! I'm just gonna make pork chops out of him!"

"That's the same thing, Dad!"

Sal nearly caught the piglet at the front

door, but luckily Megs got there first and opened it.

Oink flew through the doorway and down the sidewalk.

Sal sped after him like a robed, bunny-slippered locomotive, kids dangling from his body like Christmas ornaments.

He stomped all the way to the animal adoption agency, just in time to see Oink slip through a half-opened window.

The shelter wasn't open yet, but Sal hammered the door with his fists.

Eventually, Frida opened the door. As soon as she saw Sal, she said icily, "Oh, it's you. *Of course* it's you. Returning the pig already?" Oink cowered safely behind Frida's legs.

Sal tried to talk, but he was so mad he could only make strange strangled noises.

Finally he roared, "PEPPERS! DON'T! DO! PETS!"

In Brazil, that scientist with the radio dish looking for aliens made another notch in her notebook, this time in the *definitely maybe* category.

CHAPTER 10

"There will be no more pets in the Pepper home," Sal said. Oink had been the last straw.

Frida agreed that if the Peppers weren't going to even bother trying to properly train their pets, then they didn't deserve them anyway, and she would allow no future adoptions.

The family had had a lot of heartbreak over the past week, but somehow the loss of Oink hurt the most of all.

But as much as she'd miss the pig, Annie couldn't stop crying as she said goodbye to the dream of ever taking her beloved Azzie home.

No one spoke as they returned to the house that morning.

No one said a word all day.

No one made a sound at dinner.

It was the quietest night ever in the Pepper household.

As Annie made her way to bed, she peeked in on everyone. Sal sat at the kitchen table cradling the empty pot that he still hadn't had the will to wash. Tee reread Frida Flamingo's pamphlet in the dining room. Upstairs, Maria lay on her bed, gently ringing Lacey's cat bell.

Annie heard a single sad oboe chord coming from Ricky's room.

Beta sat at his laptop, quietly editing his movie.

"You going to bed soon, Beta?" Annie asked.

He shrugged. "Might as well. I was so close to finishing my movie, Annie. It was going to be a masterpiece." He sniffed. He had been crying, too.

"I'm really sorry, Beta," Annie said. "G'night." And she went to her room and flopped into bed.

And she *was* sorry. For all of it.

The fact was, this was all her fault.

She was the one who had convinced the family to adopt a pet.

She was the one who had let Harry loose and started the whole chain of events.

If only there was some way she could fix it. What they needed was a happy ending. But Annie knew that happy endings only happened in books and movies.

Movies! she thought. *That's it!*

A plan came to her in a flash. She knew exactly what to do. It would take some work, but she was sure she was up to the challenge.

CHAPTER 11

The family didn't see much of Annie for the next few days. She only popped up to ask a few favors.

First she asked to borrow Beta's laptop, and he readily agreed.

"What am I gonna do with it now? Play video games?"

Next she asked her
dad for his chili recipe.

"Okay. Why not?" he
answered glumly. "Not
like it's a top secret
award-winning recipe or
anything . . ." *Sigh*.

After breakfast each
morning, Annie ran out of the house and didn't
return until dinner. No one knew where she
went, or why. But then again, all the Peppers
were too down in the dumps to really care.

Then one morning, about a week after what
is now known as the Infamous Chili Incident
of '19, Sal padded into the kitchen for some
cereal. He was keenly aware that there was no
gold medal hanging around his neck.

As he reached for the milk, he realized there

was a brightly colored flyer taped to the refrigerator door.

There was one taped to Ricky's oboe. Another hung from the banister. One was stuck to the bathroom mirror. Beta found one taped to his bedpost. They all read:

COME SEE
TERRORUS
TERROR FROM BEYOND
THE STARS

1 P.M.
GOOGLEPLEX
CINEMA
!!!

STARRING SCREEN LEGEND
FRIDA FLAMINGO
AND HER AMAZING ANIMALS!

PROCEEDS BENEFIT FRIDA
FLAMINGO'S ANIMAL ADOPTION AGENCY

DIRECTED BY BETA MAX PEPPER
ASSISTANT DIRECTOR, ANNIE PEPPER

Wait, what? Beta wondered if he was still dreaming. There was no way his movie was showing today.

Annie was listed as assistant director. She had to be behind this.

At one o'clock, the Chili Chikka-Wow-Wow food truck pulled up in front of the Googleplex Cinema. As the Peppers fell out of the truck, they were shocked to see a line of people stretching around the corner. It seemed as though Annie had papered all of San Pimento with flyers for Beta's movie.

Everyone around them was chatting excitedly about the film. Frida Flamingo had been a huge action-movie star in the 1970s, but no one had heard from her in years. How exciting to see her act again!

Another surprise awaited the family when they finally reached the ticket booth. Annie was behind the counter.

"What exactly is going on, young lady?" Tee Pepper asked, gesturing wildly.

"How did you get the Googleplex Cinema to allow you to show a movie?" asked Maria.

"And how did you finish my movie?" asked Beta.

"And when did you plaster these cool flyers all over town?" asked Megs.

"Hey . . . is that girl over there checking me out?" asked Ricky (who indeed was being smiled at by a girl he recognized from history class).

"SCOOCHY WANT POPCORN! NOW!" demanded Scoochy.

"I'm not sure what you've done," Sal scolded Annie, "but I've got the feeling you are in serious trouble when we get home, young lady." He did a quick calculation. "Also, I'd like two adult and five kids' tickets, please."

"And one senior!" Meemaw piped up, whacking Sal with her cane.

The theater was crowded, but Annie had roped off seats for the family in the second row. They sat directly behind Frida Flamingo and what looked like four empty spots reserved for Frida's special guests.

"Chili! Hot chili! Get yer piping hot, tasty chili here, courtesy of Chili Chikka-Wow-Wow!"

Sal's head spun around. Standing in the aisle, six rows back, Annie's friend Marco was dishing out hot chili to theatergoers.

"Hey!" Sal cried. "What are you . . ."

"Shhhh," hissed Frida Flamingo. "The movie is about to begin. No talking! I can't stand it when people talk during movies."

There was a polite oink from the empty seat beside her.

Sal raised his eyebrows in surprise and settled into his seat as the lights went down and the movie began.

It had action. It had suspense. It had drama. Mostly it had a fifty-foot mutant tarantula-cat-bird-pig from outer space laying waste to the countryside and eating every person and automobile that got in its way.

But the biggest surprise was Frida Flamingo, whose dramatic return to film was gutsy and entertaining. She played a maverick soldier who discovered the creature's only weakness, a severe lactose intolerance. The scene where she convinced the Pentagon to create a chocolate sundae the size of a battleship was Oscar-worthy. And the final moment, when she flew a giant spoon directly into the creature's mouth and sacrificed herself, brought a tear to Sal's eye.

Beta couldn't believe it. The movie was a masterpiece.

YER ABOUT TO GET CREAMED!

Finally the film came to an end. For a moment, the audience was silent. Beta was petrified that the moviegoers had hated it, but then they broke into wild applause as Annie brought up the lights.

She ran up to the front of the house, microphone in hand.

"Thank you. Thank you all for coming today. It's my honor to introduce you to the mastermind behind this film, my brother Beta Max Pepper. Take a bow, Beta!"

Beta stood and waved bashfully.

"We couldn't have done it without the amazing talents of Frida Flamingo, in her triumphant comeback. And, of course, we also have to thank the real stars of the movie. Please put your hands together for Frida Flamingo's Amazing Animals!"

Annie waved to Oink, who oinked happily at the crowd. He and the other animals had been hiding in the seats next to Frida all along.

Harry waved at the crowd from his terrarium
with all eight legs. Lacey yawned, clearly unim-
pressed. Elvis the lovebird chirped, *Thank you,
thank you very much!*

"And just so you know, all the animals at
Frida Flamingo's Animal Shelter are available
for adoption! Please find it in your hearts to
take one into your home. Thank you!" The
crowd clapped again as Marco walked up and
down the aisle, handing out pamphlets.

Beta ran up to Annie. "But . . . but . . . how did you do it all, Annie? The movie is so good!"

Annie blushed.

"It was your sister's idea to show the movie as a benefit for the shelter," Frida said, joining them. "She suggested we call in a little help to finish it."

Just then, a man with graying hair, a beard, and glasses walked over. He pointed to Annie and said, "This bright young lady convinced Frida to call me. I owed Frida a favor, after all. She got me my first job at Looniversal Pictures."

Beta's jaw dropped. It was the famous movie director Stevie Shpealburger!

The director smiled at Beta. "You gave me

some great material to work with, kid. You have quite the bright future. Maybe someday we can do a movie together."

"Uhh duhh uhh."

Beta was so dumbstruck that his tongue wouldn't work.

A couple of men licking their spoons cornered Sal. "Are you the owner of the Chili Chikka-Wow-Wow truck?"

"That's me," Sal replied worriedly.

"Well, we're two of the judges from the annual San Pimento Chili Cook-Off, and we have to say, you should definitely enter next year!" One of the judges leaned in and whispered to Sal, "Between you and me, this is ten times better than the chili that won first prize! You'd be a shoo-in!"

Sal beamed from ear to ear.

CHAPTER 12

Annie confessed to everything. She had run over to Frida Flamingo's with the wild idea to finish Beta's movie and show it to the town so they would adopt the animals. Then Annie had found Stevie Shpealburger's phone number and convinced Frida to call him to help finish the film.

While Frida and Mr. Shpealburger filmed and edited the final scenes, Annie and Marco had cooked up a fresh batch of Sal's nearly award-winning chili!

"Well, it looks like you're a real hero, Annie!" said Tee.

Annie shook her head. "I'm no hero. I'm ter-rible! I was so jealous of Beta that I let Harry out of the cage. It's *my* fault Beta lost his pet. He should get Harry back."

Beta scratched his head. "Well," he admitted, "I may have spritzed Lacey with that lavender perfume to drive Elvis crazy as revenge for losing Harry. It's really Maria and Ricky who should get their pets back."

Maria and Ricky looked at each other. "Um, Maria and I were so upset about losing Lacey and Elvis that we let Oink loose in the kitchen overnight. Sorry, Dad," said Ricky. "Sorry, Megs."

Maria added, "We'll help you win that chili title next year."

Ricky nodded. "We solemnly swear to!"

Megs shrugged. "Well, I didn't break any Pepper rules, but I still feel awful. Too many helpings of chili!"

They all laughed and had a giant Pepper family hug, with Annie at the center.

"You know what? Peppers don't do rules!" Sal cried. "At least, not all the time. But we DO do pets! In fact, the Peppers are re-adopting them all! Even that pig!"

Megs snickered. "Dad said *doo doo* again!"

Maria rolled her eyes.

Frida wagged her finger at Sal. "Fine, I'll let you have them back because your daughter has such a big heart. And so, it seems, do you. But you can't just go returning pets whenever they do something wrong. You have to *train* them!"

Sal looked down at his shoes shyly. "Yes, ma'am."

"You know, this was really all Annie's idea to begin with," said Megs. "It's not exactly fair that she never got a chance to adopt the pet she wanted. I'd have been angry, too."

Tee turned to Annie. "What pet did you want, sweetie?"

As if on cue, Azzie the Chihuahua came

running down the theater aisle and leapt right into Annie's arms. "Azzie!" Annie laughed. "Where did you come from?"

Azzie looked nervously at the door, where a gang of mean-looking squirrels gathered, cracking nuts and looking tough.

Annie put Azzie down and rolled up her sleeves. "Azzie may not have been ready for you last time, squirrels, but now he's got a posse . . . a *Pepper* posse. You ready, guys?"

Oink stood beside her and oinked menacingly. Lacey hissed in French and opened Harry's cage. Elvis ran a comb through his nonexistent pompadour and sneered. Annie's brothers and sisters stood behind her.

119

"You mess with one Pepper, you mess with us all," said Megs.

"And Azzie's one of us now," growled Beta.

It was an *epic* battle. Luckily Mr. Shpealburger had brought his camera along and got it all on tape. It even inspired his next Oscar-winning film, *Battle at Squirrel Beach*, featuring Frida Flamingo's return to the big screen.

The Peppers were all invited to the premiere. And Azzie the Chihuahua sat on Annie's lap the whole time.

The End?*

*No! The Peppers will be back! In *The Pepper Party Family Feud Face-Off*!

121

Can't get enough Pepper pandemonium? Read on for a sneak peek of this feisty family's next crazy catastrophe!

All over San Pimento, people watching the competition on live television broke into fits of laughter. They giggled and snorted and chortled and guffawed. Some even laughed so hard that they peed a little. If they happened to be drinking milk, it poured through their noses.

It was Maria's worst nightmare. Except this was really happening. Her family had embarrassed her more than anyone had ever been embarrassed in the history of the universe. Her face red with humiliation and tomatoes, she finally made it to her feet and shouted into the microphone:

"THAT'S IT! I QUIT!!!"

The students in the auditorium went quiet. Ms. Macaroon walked delicately out to the stage. "You mean, you quit the competition?"

Maria turned to her, fury blazing in her eyes. "No. *I quit the Peppers.*"

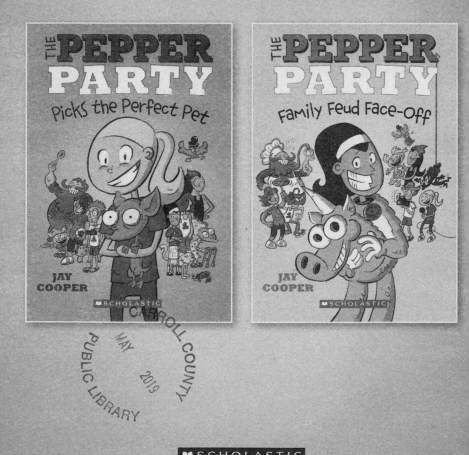